Too Far Away to Touch

Too Far Away to Touch

by Lesléa Newman
illustrated by Catherine Stock

Clarion Books ★ New York

A portion of the proceeds from this book will be donated to AIDS organizations.

Clarion Books • a Houghton Mifflin Company imprint • 215 Park Avenue South, New York, NY 10003 • Text copyright © 1995 by Lesléa Newman • Illustrations copyright © 1995 by Catherine Stock • The illustrations for this book were executed in watercolor on Saunders watercolor paper. • The text was set in 14/19 pt. Sabon. • All rights reserved. • For information about permission to reproduce selections from this book, write to Permissions, Houghton Mifflin Company, 215 Park Avenue South, New York, NY 10003. • Printed in Singapore

Library of Congress Cataloging-in-Publication Data
Newman, Lesléa.   Too far away to touch / by Lesléa Newman ; illustrated by Catherine Stock.
p. cm.   Summary: Zoe's favorite uncle Leonard takes her to a planetarium and explains that if he dies he will be like the stars, too far away to touch, close enough to see. ISBN 0-395-68968-6   [1. AIDS (Disease)—Fiction. 2. Uncles—Fiction. 3. Death—Fiction. 4. Stars—Fiction.]   I. Stock, Catherine, ill. II. Title.   PZ7.N47988To 1995   [E]—dc20 93-30327   CIP   AC

TWP 10 9 8 7 6 5 4 3 2 1

IN MEMORY OF GERARD RIZZA
(*1959–1992*)

"A star
is as far
as the eye
can see
and
as near
as my eye
is to me"
—*Gregory Corso,*
"Proximity"

—L. N.

For B
supernova in my night sky.

—C.

Whenever Uncle Leonard comes to visit, he takes me on a great adventure, like to the Museum of Modern Art or the Bronx Zoo.

We hadn't seen him in a long time, but then he called and said he was coming to take me to the Hayden Planetarium.

I was sitting in the living room waiting for him with two marbles in my hand, a blue one and a green one, because I was going to play a trick on him. When Uncle Leonard came, I was going to pat his woolly head, open my hand, and say, "Look, Uncle Leonard, you're losing your marbles!"

I couldn't wait to hear his big booming laugh.

When the doorbell rang, I yelled, "I'll get it."

I ran and opened the door without even looking through the peephole like I'm supposed to.

"Hi, Uncle Leonard."

"Hi, Zoe."

Uncle Leonard squatted down to hug me, but he was wearing a black beret, so I couldn't play my trick on him yet.

"Where's Nathan?" I asked, putting my marbles back in my pocket as Uncle Leonard stood up.

"He had to work today," Uncle Leonard said, "so it's just me and you."

"C'mon." I ran to press the button for the elevator.

"Have fun, you two." Mom waved to us from the doorway. "Zoe, don't tire your uncle out."

"I won't," I said right as the elevator came.

Uncle Leonard hailed a taxi to take us all the way up to West Eighty-first Street. When we stopped at a red light, Uncle Leonard leaned his head back against the seat and closed his eyes. But as soon as we started going he opened them again.

"Hey Zoe, guess which hand?" He put his two fists out in front of me.

I pointed. "Right."

"Wrong." He opened his right hand and it was empty.

"Left."

"Right." He opened his left hand and there was a folded-up five-dollar bill in it for the taxi driver.

"Now Zoe," Uncle Leonard said, "how can my right hand be my wrong hand and my left hand be my right hand?"

I thought about it for a minute but then Uncle Leonard laughed, so I knew he was teasing me. I started to laugh, but then Uncle Leonard stopped laughing and started coughing, so I stopped laughing too.

When we got to the Planetarium, we saw a sign that said a show was just about to start.

"We're in luck," Uncle Leonard said as he bought our tickets.

We went inside and scrunched down low in our seats so we could look up at the ceiling. I didn't even have time to take my marbles out of my pocket before all the lights went out and it was dark as night. I couldn't see anything, but I heard a low whirring noise. Suddenly, a shooting star zoomed across the ceiling and everyone gasped.

Then all at once the dark above us was lit up with a million, billion, trillion shining stars. There were moons and planets too. A man's voice told us all about the sky. He called it the heavens.

"How far away are the stars?" I whispered to Uncle Leonard.

"Too far away to touch, but close enough to see," he whispered back.

When the show was over, all the lights came on and I blinked a few times. "That was really great," I said as Uncle Leonard and I climbed the steps. "I wish I could see all the stars like that every night. All I see outside my window is the big brick building next door."

"I have an idea," Uncle Leonard said. He took me to the Planetarium Gift Shop and told me to wait over by the picture books. I looked at some pictures of Saturn and Jupiter until he came back with a brown paper bag.

"What's in there?" I asked, but Uncle Leonard wouldn't tell me.

"A surprise" is all he said.

"Want to get something to eat?" Uncle Leonard asked when we were out on the street again.

"Okay," I answered. Then I remembered what Mom had said in the hallway. "But are you sure you're not too tired?"

"I'm all right," said Uncle Leonard. "Look, there's a café right here."

We went inside and sat down at a little round table. I ordered my very favorite dessert, a double fudge chocolate-chip brownie and a big glass of milk, and Uncle Leonard asked for a cup of lemon tea. I took my marbles out of my pocket and held them under the table, waiting, but Uncle Leonard didn't take off his beret.

Finally I asked him, "Aren't you going to take off your hat?"

"Oh, right," Uncle Leonard said, almost like he'd forgotten he had it on.

He reached up and I started to slide off my seat, but then
I stopped because when Uncle Leonard pulled off his beret
I saw that his fluffy cloud of hair was gone. Instead he only had
short wispy tufts sticking out in different directions, and in some
places I could even see the pink shiny skin of his head.

"What happened?" I asked, slipping the marbles back into my pocket. They made a soft little clink.

"It's part of being sick," Uncle Leonard said, putting his beret back on.

Just then the waiter came back with our order and Uncle Leonard's watch beeped.

"Time for my medicine," Uncle Leonard said. "That's part of being sick too."

I watched him swallow a yellow pill with his tea.

"Does it hurt?" I asked.

"No," he answered with a smile, but it was a sad kind of smile.

"Are you getting better?"

"No," he said, "I'm about the same."

I took a bite of my brownie, but it tasted like mud.

"Are you going to get better soon?"

"I don't know, Zoe."

Uncle Leonard patted my hand and sighed a long, deep sigh. I squeezed his hand tight and he squeezed mine back.

When we got home, Mom was in the kitchen chopping up cucumbers for a salad.

"Help your mother, and don't come into your room until I call you," Uncle Leonard said, heading down the hallway with his paper bag.

"What's he going to do?" I asked Mom, but she just shrugged and handed me a tomato to wash.

Soon Uncle Leonard called out, "Ready."
Mom and I raced down the hall to my room.
Uncle Leonard held out his hand and said, "Look, Zoe."
There in the center of his palm was a tiny white star.
"Keep your eye on that star," Uncle Leonard said as he shut off the light.
The room turned pitch black and the star glowed and twinkled just like it was real. "Now, look up," he said, reaching out his hand.

I stretched my head back and gasped.

Uncle Leonard had pasted glow-in-the-dark stars all over my ceiling.

It looked just like the Planetarium!

"Oh," Mom said, "how beautiful."

"Know how far away the stars are, Mom?" I asked, reaching up with both hands. "Too far away to touch, but close enough to see. Right, Uncle Leonard?"

Uncle Leonard didn't answer, so Mom turned on the light and we saw that he had fallen asleep on my bed.

"Shh," Mom said, turning off the light again. "Don't wake him up, Zoe. Go get a blanket from my bed."

I got Mom's blue striped afghan and she smoothed it out over Uncle Leonard. He didn't even wake up when Mom took off his shoes.

I didn't see Uncle Leonard for a while after that, but I talked to him on the phone.

"Do you still like the stars in your room?" he asked. His voice sounded soft and fuzzy, as if he'd just been sleeping.

"They're great," I said, "but I wish I could see all the stars in the sky for real."

"I have an idea," Uncle Leonard said. "As soon as I feel a little stronger, we're going to go on another adventure."

Two Saturdays later, Uncle Leonard called and told me to be ready at five o'clock. He and Nathan picked me up in Nathan's car. Uncle Leonard was wearing a baseball cap.

"Are we going to a baseball game?" I asked, but they wouldn't tell me.

"You'll see," Nathan said.

"It's a surprise," said Uncle Leonard.

Nathan drove us out of the city and onto the highway. Soon the air made my nose all tingly with its salty ocean smell. We stopped and ate supper at Captain Jack's, this seafood restaurant that had all kinds of fish and fishing nets and a lobster trap hanging on a wall. Nathan and I had fish and chips and Uncle Leonard had a cup of soup.

Then when it was almost dark, Nathan drove us to the beach. We put a blanket on the sand, stretched out, and waited.

Soon it was completely dark and all the stars came out one by one by one.

A cool breeze blew and I snuggled up close to Uncle Leonard.

Nathan took off his jacket. "Put this on," he said to Uncle Leonard. "I'll go back to the car and see if we have another blanket."

I listened to Nathan's footsteps in the sand until I couldn't hear them anymore. All I could hear were the waves of the ocean tumbling in and out. And all I could see were stars and stars and stars. The sky looked so big, I felt very small and a little lonely, even though my uncle was right there next to me.

"Why did the man in the Planetarium call the sky the heavens?" I asked Uncle Leonard.

"I don't know, Zoe."

"Is that where people go when they die?"

"Maybe."

"Are you going to die, Uncle Leonard?" I looked at his face in the moonlight.

Uncle Leonard didn't answer for a minute, but I felt his hand squeeze my shoulder tight.

"Everyone has to die sometime, Zoe," he said. "There is no cure for AIDS yet, so I may die soon. But I hope not. I'd like to live for a long, long time."

I looked up at the stars again. "But where will you go when you die?"

"I don't know where I'll go," Uncle Leonard said, "but I know where I'll be. Too far away to touch, but close enough to see."

As soon as he said it, I knew he was right, because even with my eyes closed I could picture Uncle Leonard sitting at the café near the Planetarium, smiling his sad kind of smile.

"Zoe, Leonard, look quick." Nathan's voice was loud in the dark. "Look to the right. A shooting star!"

I turned my head, and saw the tip of the shooting star vanish.

Nathan came to us and covered Uncle Leonard's shoulders with a blanket. "Did you see it?"

"Yes," Uncle Leonard said, "but it disappeared so fast."

"But it's not gone," I whispered, shutting my eyes. And there was the shooting star again, too far away to touch, but close enough to see.